A walk in the rain

by Ursel Scheffler • pictures by Ulises Wensell

translated by Andrea Mernan

G. P. Putnam's Sons

New York

J osh loved visiting his grandparents, especially on rainy days. Because Josh's grandmother loved to walk in the rain.

Josh loved to walk in the rain, too. But he always got soaking wet.

"We'll have to get you a raincoat," his grandmother said as she wrapped him in a big blue towel.

The next time Josh visited, his grandmother gave him a bright yellow raincoat with a matching hat. And his grandfather gave him a pair of shiny rubber boots. Josh tried them on right away, but it didn't rain for weeks.

Finally one morning Josh heard raindrops
pattering against his window. He could hardly wait
to go for a walk.

The rain dripped on his new raincoat. It gushed
around the rim of his hat. Josh splashed through all
the puddles in his shiny rubber boots.

He found a ladybug and gently put her on the branch
of a bush where the leaves could shelter her from the rain.
"Granny," he asked, "where do the birds go when it rains?"

"Let's find out," his grandmother said.

They found birds in the trees. They found birds under windowsills. Josh even spotted some way up high under the roof of a house.

When they found two little sparrows perched on a
fence, Josh said, "Look, Granny! They need raincoats too!"
But Josh's grandmother explained that birds' feathers
are covered with oil, which helps keep them dry in the
rain just like a raincoat.

Josh found a pile of leaves that had collected near a drain, making a dam. He poked a hole in the leaves, and the water gurgled down the drain.

When they came to a
stream, Josh threw a twig in
the water and watched it
WOOSH away.

Then they crossed the
bridge and went into the
woods, where someone had
cut down some trees.

Josh and his grandmother climbed onto the
logs and pretended they were tightrope walkers.

By the time they climbed down, Barney had disappeared. They called and they whistled. They whistled and they called. But they didn't see Barney anywhere.

"He's probably off chasing rabbits," Grandmother decided.

Josh whistled one more time as loudly as he could, and Barney came running back. He was covered with mud from top to tail.

"I think it's time to go home," Grandmother said.

On the way home, Josh looked for mushrooms.
"They sprout everywhere when it rains," his
grandmother told him. Josh counted seven growing
by a tree.

When they got home, Josh's grandmother hung
their raincoats over the bathtub, while Josh and his
grandfather rubbed Barney dry.

Then Josh told everyone about all the things he had seen during his walk in the rain.

Afterward, Josh watched the rain splash against the window while his grandfather read him a story. That was another reason Josh loved rainy days.

Library of Congress Cataloging in Publication Data
Scheffler, Ursel.   A walk in the rain.
Translation of: Spatzen Brauchen keinen Schirm.
Summary: Josh goes for a walk in the rain with
his grandmother and wears his new rainwear.
1. Children's stories, German. [1. Rain and
rainfall—Fiction.   2. Grandmothers—Fiction]
I. Wensell, Ulises, ill.   II. Title.
PZ7.S3425Wal   1986   [E]   85-5684
ISBN 0-399-21267-1